Disney CHANNEL
ROC

By Emma Harrison and Kieran Viola

"High School Musical" is based on the Disney Channel Original Movie, Written by Peter Barsocchini

"High School Musical 2" is based on the Disney Channel Original Movie, Written by Peter Barsocchini
Based on Characters Created by Peter Barsocchini

"Cory in the House" is based on the series created by Marc Warren & Dennis Rinsler

"The Suite Life of Zack & Cody" is based on the series created by Danny Kallis & Jim Geoghan

"Hannah Montana" is based on the series created by Michael Poryes and Rich Correll & Barry O'Brien

"Wizards of Waverly Place" is based on the series created by Todd J. Greenwald

"Camp Rock" is based on the Disney Channel Original Movie,
Written by Karin Gist & Regina Hicks and Julie Brown & Paul Brown

"Phineas and Ferb" is based on the series created by Dan Povenmire and Jeff "Swampy" Marsh

DISNEY
PRESS

New York

All recipes originally ran in *Family Fun* magazine. *FamilyFun* is a division of the Walt Disney Publishing Group. To order a subscription, call 800-289-4849.

Printed in the United States of America

First Edition

1 3 5 7 9 10 8 6 4 2

Library of Congress Catalog Card Number: 2007909628

ISBN 978-1-4231-1321-8

For more Disney Press fun, visit www.disneybooks.com

Visit DisneyChannel.com

LET THE GOOD TIMES ROLL!

What's the first word that comes to mind when you think of the Disney Channel? Stars? Music? Excitement? How about: fun, fun, fun! (Okay, that's one word three times, but we just couldn't help ourselves.)

Well, why should the fun end when you turn off your TV? It shouldn't! That's why we've put together this special book full of quizzes, trivia, recipes, and the latest lowdown about all your favorite Disney Channel shows and stars!

Think you know all there is to know about *High School Musical*? Find out with our Wildcats quiz! Curious to learn fun facts about *Hannah Montana* or *The Suite Life of Zack & Cody*? Scope out our trivia sections. Want to learn how to make awesome Wildcat Burritos or Cory's tasty chicken cutlets? Check out our awesome recipes. Feel the need to read all about *Wizards of Waverly Place* and its stars? We've got you covered. Plus, you get an extra glimpse into some of the Disney Channel's newest hits, like *Camp Rock* and *Phineas & Ferb*!

It's all in this insider's guide. So what are you waiting for? Jump in!

HIGH SCHOOL MUSICAL

HIGH SCHOOL MUSICAL 2

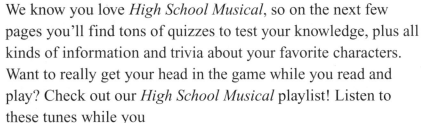

We know you love *High School Musical*, so on the next few pages you'll find tons of quizzes to test your knowledge, plus all kinds of information and trivia about your favorite characters. Want to really get your head in the game while you read and play? Check out our *High School Musical* playlist! Listen to these tunes while you read, and you'll be so in the zone that not even a cell phone could distract you.

HIGH SCHOOL MUSICAL PLAYLIST

1. "Start of Something New"
2. "Get'cha Head in the Game"
3. "What I've Been Looking For"
4. "Stick to the Status Quo"
5. "When There Was Me and You"
6. "Bop to the Top"
7. "Breaking Free"
8. "We're All in This Together"

TROY BOLTON

Troy was the first sophomore to make the East High Wildcats varsity basketball team. His teammates unanimously elected him captain junior year, and he went on to lead the squad to a stellar season, bringing them back to the district championship game for the first time in three years. (Go Wildcats!)

But Troy also surprised everyone, from his classmates to his teachers to his family (and maybe even himself), when he auditioned for the winter musical, *Twinkle Towne*, and won the male lead! Who knew Troy Bolton, man of many skills on the basketball court, could actually sing? He not only brought down the house during his audition with Gabriella Montez, but he also gave incredible performances in three straight sold-out shows.

That summer, Troy attended basketball camp with the Wildcats for two weeks and then landed a job at Lava Springs Country Club, where in no time he was promoted from busboy to golf teacher and caddy. He also participated in the club's Midsummer Night's Star Dazzle Talent Show and stole the spotlight once again, singing a duet with—who else—Gabriella. Looks like Troy might be a superstar in the making!

GABRIELLA MONTEZ

Gabriella is relatively new to East High, and at first it looked as if she was content to just lay low and blend in. But that changed pretty quickly when Sharpay Evans uncovered Gabriella's secret Einstein-ette past, and Taylor McKessie recruited her for the Scholastic Decathlon team. Thanks to Gabriella's sharp pen and even sharper mind, East High crushed their rival, West High, in the biggest academic showdown of the year!

Little did anyone know that Gabriella wasn't just a bookworm. A member of her church choir for years, Gabriella decided to try out for the winter musical and won the female lead. For the first time since anyone at East High could remember, someone other than Sharpay Evans got top billing in a Drama Club production. Singing obviously brings this girl all kinds of joy, and that joy was infectious during the three sold-out performances of *Twinkle Towne*.

Over the summer, Gabriella landed a job as a lifeguard at Lava Springs Country Club, where she paired up with Troy Bolton in the Midsummer Night's Star Dazzle Talent Show. Once again, they brought down the house. Not that anyone was surprised. Everything that sweet Gabriella touches turns to gold!

SHARPAY EVANS

Sharpay is one of those people who knows who she is and is not afraid to flaunt it. She has been a fashion plate and dramatic superstar ever since kindergarten. She has won the starring role in every play and musical East High has staged since she was a freshman. That's probably why she was so incredibly freaked out when she heard Gabriella Montez sing. It was the first time Sharpay faced any real competition.

Of course, Sharpay found a creative way to deal with it. At her suggestion, Ms. Darbus moved the callbacks so that they would take place at the same time as Troy's championship basketball game *and* Gabriella's Scholastic Decathlon match. But by some crazy freak accident (wink, wink), both Troy and Gabriella's events were put on hold and they were able to perform after all. In the end, Gabriella won the lead and Sharpay was forced to take a supporting role.

But Sharpay wasn't down for long. That summer, she got the manager of her country club to offer Troy a job, then she landed him a meeting with the coach from the University of Albuquerque basketball team and *then* tricked him into agreeing to sing with her in the club's talent show. That all backfired when Troy realized what she was up to, but don't worry about Sharpay—that girl always has something up her designer sleeve.

CHAD DANFORTH

Anyone who has met Chad knows he's all about basketball. He would do anything for the team, including trying to convince Troy Bolton not to audition for the winter musical.

Chad wanted Troy to stay focused on the championship basketball game, so that the Wildcats could bring home the trophy. In fact, he was so persuasive that he almost robbed East High of watching Troy star in *Twinkle Towne*. Fortunately, he realized he was wrong just in time, and instead of sabotaging Troy, Chad ended up helping him get his callback. We love a guy who can admit when he's made a mistake.

Of course, it was no coincidence that Chad had just started to notice the charms of a certain brainiac, Taylor McKessie. Before Troy and Gabriella shook things up, Chad never would have noticed Taylor, but now, well, he's *definitely* taken an interest. And that summer, they got to spend all kinds of time together, working at the Lava Springs Country Club. Chad saved up all his paychecks to put toward his very own car. Looks like he and Taylor and their friends could be riding to East High in style next year!

RYAN EVANS

It's hard to imagine Ryan without his sister, Sharpay. The two of them share everything, from a love of the theater, to a wealth of talent, to the co-presidency of the Drama Club. These two must have been born with microphones in their hands! Like Sharpay, Ryan has won the lead in every Drama Club production he's auditioned for (except for the winter musical, of course).

When it comes to fashion, Ryan has a style all his own. (What other guy at East High owns as many hats as Ryan?) When it comes to *scheming*, Sharpay is the brains of the Evans' operation. But Ryan has always stood by her side, ready to help in any way he can.

That summer, when it came time for Sharpay to choose a singing partner for the Lava Springs Country Club's talent show, she dumped Ryan and went with Troy. Totally betrayed, Ryan went out and found himself some new people to hang out with—the rest of the East High Wildcats! Ryan helped them choreograph their own routine and realized that he can do pretty well without his bossy sister. In the end, even Sharpay noticed how talented her brother was and gave him the coveted Star Dazzle award. You go, Ryan!

TAYLOR MCKESSIE

Taylor McKessie is the smartest girl at East High. She maintains a straight A average while leading the Scholastic Decathlon team. It had always been Taylor's dream to get the East High team past the first round of the Scholastic Decathlon competition. So as soon as Taylor found out that new girl Gabriella Montez was something of a brainiac, she recruited her for the team. Together, those two smarties led their squad to their first-ever Scholastic Decathlon victory. Go, girls!

Up until she met her new BFF Gabriella, Taylor admits she was something of an intelli-snob. She thought all student athletes were on the dim side, but thanks to Gabriella, Taylor got to know Troy Bolton, Chad Danforth, and their friends, and now she can be seen hanging out with all types of people—as long as they don't cut into her study time.

That summer, Taylor was in charge of member activities at the Lava Springs Country Club—a very senior job for someone as young as she is. But that's Taylor for you—always excelling at everything she does. Who would expect anything less?

FRIENDS 4EVER!

So you've seen *High School Musical* 423 times (give or take a few). You know all the dance moves and can hit all the notes. You know that Troy is the captain of the varsity basketball team and that Gabriella once won a trophy for her science skills. Maybe you even know that Sharpay and Ryan are the co-presidents of the Drama Club. But are you a true East High Wildcat? Better get your head in the game, because we're about to test your *High School Musical* knowledge, big-time.

1. When Gabriella's mom tells her to go to the New Year's Eve party, what is Gabriella doing?
   A. Chatting with friends
   B. Reading a book
   C. Watching the fire in the fireplace

2. What technology does Ms. Darbus call "a menace"?
   A. DVD players
   B. Alarm clocks
   C. Cell phones

3. What are the Wildcats' school colors?
   A. Red and white
   B. Red and orange
   C. Red and blue

4. Why do Gabriella and her mom move to Albuquerque?
   A. Mrs. Montez's company moves her there.
   B. Gabriella didn't like her old school.
   C. Gabriella wanted to go to school with Troy.

5. On her first day at East High, what is Gabriella afraid of becoming?
   A. The school outcast
   B. The school's freaky genius girl
   C. The school drama queen

6. Ryan and Sharpay are:
   A. Cousins
   B. Brother and sister
   C. Archenemies

ANSWERS:

1. B **2. C** **3. A**

4. A **5. B** **6. B**

SCORING

Give yourself two points for each correct answer. If you scored:

0-4

GET'CHA HEAD IN THE GAME!

Maybe another viewing of *High School Musical* will get your Wildcat pride pumping!

6-8

YOU'VE GOT SOME WILDCAT SPIRIT!

You know the basics, but you might want to hit the books before taking another Wildcat quiz!

10-12

YOU'RE A TRUE WILDCAT!

You clearly know a lot about East High and its students. Now check out the rest of our *High School Musical* quizzes to see if you can keep the pride alive!

SUMMER FUN

Happy summer vacation, Wildcats! You've sailed through the first Wildcat quiz, all made up of questions from *High School Musical*. Now grab your Lava Springs Country Club employee handbook, because the next quiz will test your knowledge of *High School Musical 2*!

1. The Wildcats' boss at the country club is named:
   A. Mr. Johnson
   B. Mr. Fulton
   C. Mr. Bolton

2. What is Gabriella's job at the country club?
   A. Lifeguard
   B. Waitress
   C. Babysitter

3. In *High School Musical 2* we find out that Troy played what sport, aside from basketball, during the school year?
   A. Football
   B. Tennis
   C. Golf

4. Whose family founded the country club?
   A. Troy's
   B. Kelsi's
   C. Sharpay and Ryan's

5. What type of production does Sharpay put on every summer at the country club?
   A. A musical
   B. A talent show
   C. A rock concert

6. Who does Sharpay think is East High's "primo boy"?
   A. Troy
   B. Zeke
   C. Ryan

7. How does Troy get his job at the country club?
   A. He applies for it.
   B. Sharpay gets him hired.
   C. His dad recommends him.

ANSWERS:

1.B **2.A** **3.C** **4.C**

5.B **6.A** **7.B**

SCORING

Give yourself two points for each correct answer. If you scored:

YOU'RE SCRUBBING THE POOL!
0-4 With a score like that, you get the sorriest job at the club.
Don't forget your sunscreen and cleaning supplies!

YOU'RE ON WAITSTAFF.
6-10 Not too shabby. You can be a waiter or waitress—which also
means you get to race on the dinner carts during your break.

YOU'RE A GOLF PRO!
12-14 Join Troy out there on the green! You deserve a cushy job
with a score as choice as yours.

HIGH SCHOOL MUSICAL TRIVIA!

So you've just aced your *High School Musical* and *High School Musical 2* exams. Want to know even more? You'll flip for these fab facts about the movies and cast!

17.2 million viewers watched the U.S. TV premiere of *High School Musical 2*, making it one of the most successful basic cable broadcasts in U.S. history!

In 2007, *High School Musical 2* won the award for Choice TV Movie at the Teen Choice Awards.

Corbin Bleu, who plays Chad Danforth, released his first solo album in May 2007.

Zac Efron, who plays Troy Bolton, had a starring role in 2007's cinematic summer smash *Hairspray* and will star in the upcoming feature film *Seventeen*.

Lucas Grabeel, who plays Ryan Evans, has appeared in two of the four *Halloweentown* Disney Channel Original Movies.

Both Ashley Tisdale and Vanessa Anne Hudgens (who play Sharpay Evans and Gabriella Montez) released their own solo albums in 2006.

Monique Coleman, who plays Taylor McKessie, was a contestant on ABC's *Dancing With the Stars*.

High School Musical broke the Guinness World Record for most successful songs from one soundtrack.

In 2007, Zac Efron won the Kids' Choice Award for Best Male Actor.

Corbin Bleu starred in the Disney Channel Original Movie *Jump In!* The premiere was watched by 8.2 million viewers!

High School Musical 3 will hit the big screen in October 2008!

We all know that breakfast is the most important meal of the day. But between classes, music rehearsals, and team practice, what's a student to do? Well, whip up a Wildcat Breakfast Burrito, of course! It's the perfect Southwest-inspired meal to grab on the go! But before making this, or any of the other delicious Disney Channel recipes, remember the following:

- Before you begin cooking, wash your hands and put on an apron.

- *Always* ask an adult for help when using mixers, stoves, ovens, knives, and other sharp objects.

- *Never* touch a hot stove!

WILDCAT BREAKFAST BURRITO

INGREDIENTS

1	tablespoon butter	
6	eggs, beaten	
4 to 6	eight-inch flour tortillas	

FILLING OPTIONS

1/2	cup grated cheese
1	plum tomato, chopped
1	small onion, diced
1/4	green or red pepper, chopped
1/2	avocado, diced
	Salsa
	Sliced olives
	Chopped cooked sausage, bacon, or turkey

DIRECTIONS

Over medium-high heat, melt the butter in a large, nonstick frying pan and scramble the eggs to your liking. Meanwhile, warm the tortillas for a few minutes on the rack of a 250° oven, then fill with the eggs and your choice of ingredients. Fold into a burrito as follows:

1. Fold the short end of the burrito up, so nothing spills out the bottom.
2. Fold one of the long sides on top of the filling.
3. Use your fingers to cup the tortilla over the filling and push against the filling to make a tight fold.
4. Wrap the other long end over the two folds.
5. Lay the burrito with the folded side down and let it sit for a couple of minutes so that everything sticks together. It's less messy that way!

Makes 4 burritos.

CHEF ZEKE'S TIP

You can prep the veggies the night before and store them in the fridge until you need them, saving you even more time. (Except for the avocado, which should be diced right before serving.)

HIGH SCHOOL MUSICAL

READY, SET, GRADUATE!

Are you eagerly awaiting the theatrical release of *High School Musical 3*, scheduled to hit theaters in October 2008? Of course you are! The Wildcats are gearing up for their senior year and have so many fun things to look forward to—the spring musical, the prom, and, of course, graduation day! Here's a look back on some of the fun and excitement from the first two movies.

This could be the start of something new....

Kelsi always hits just the right notes.

"We're all in this together!"

Sing it, Ryan!

Sharpay's ready!

The Wildcats get
their heads in
the game!

HIGH SCHOOL MUSICAL 2

SO MANY MEMORIES!

The Wildcats had one crazy summer at the Lava Springs Country Club! The memories they made will last forever—playing softball, picnics, barbecues, and who could forget the talent show!

The summer fun has just begun!

Play it again, Kelsi!

"Slide home, you score!"

"You are the music in me!"

"I need a little fabulous, is that so wrong?"

"Here's to right now!"

Cory Baxter

Cory always has something up his sleeve, whether it's a get-rich-quick scheme, a crazy stunt for attention, or a plot to earn the fame he knows he deserves. He had plenty of adventures back home in San Francisco, and now that his father, Victor, has landed a job as the White House chef, he has a whole new world to explore. A superposh private school packed with new and interesting friends from around the world? Check. A brand-new city where exciting events are always being held? Check. And then, of course, there's living under the same roof as President Martinez! There are so many opportunities for fun and adventure, even Cory has trouble keeping up with it all!

Unfortunately, he can't spend every minute hatching new schemes. At home, Cory has the president's daughter, Sophie, wheedling him into attending tea parties and playing games. Plus, he has President Martinez's personal assistant, Samantha Samuels, keeping him and his plans as far away from the president as possible. Not to mention that Cory's father is super busy catering to the president's and Sophie's every nutritional whim—and making Cory promise not to cause trouble. What's a fun-seeker to do?

Make friends, of course! Cory has no trouble in that department. Before long, he's landed not only a best friend in Newt Livingston but has developed a crush on Meena Parook, the free-spirited daughter of the Bahavian Ambassador. Of course, Cory is too nervous to reveal his feelings, so he and Meena become fast friends instead. With Newt, they form their own band called DC-3 and start landing gigs all over Washington, D.C. It's not all smooth sailing, though. Along the way, Cory has to help Meena live her double life as both a cool American teen and a traditional Bahavian girl, and also try to help wannabe rock star Newt avoid becoming like his stodgy politician parents. A friend's work is never done!

But don't worry. Cory won't let any of this get in the way of his plans for success. He's in the nation's capital now, a town filled with some of the most powerful people in the world, and Cory is going to find his groove and get ahead. No matter what!

Meena Parook

Meena is the very first girl Cory met at his new school, and they became instant friends. The daughter of the Bahavian Ambassador, Meena is torn between her duty to her father and country, and her love of American music, American clothing, American food . . . basically she loves anything American! Meena is the lead singer in DC-3 and loves to rock out whenever possible. She would also do anything for her friends, especially her best friends, Cory and Newt, just like they would for her.

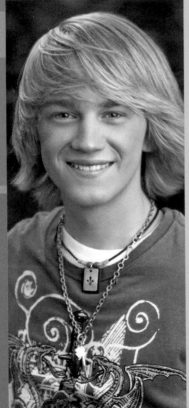

Newt Livingston

Newt seems to live a charmed life. He's handsome, comes from a rich and powerful family, and plays a mean guitar in DC-3. Problem is, Newt's dad is a senator and his mom is a Supreme Court judge. They expect Newt to follow in their footsteps, but he has zero interest in politics. He'd rather blaze his own trail—right into the Rock and Roll Hall of Fame!

Sometimes Newt is torn between the life he's supposed to have and the one he wants, but most of the time he doesn't let it bother him. He'd rather hang out with his best friends, Cory and Meena, and play some tunes. Newt can deal with the future later. For now, it's his world, and he's just rocking it!

Victor Baxter

Cory's father was a well-known chef back in San Francisco, but who would have thought that a bowl of gumbo would land him a job as the White House chef? When President Martinez visited the Chill Grill, he knew that he had found his cook. Now Victor has a full plate—from preparing White House dinners to keeping Cory out of trouble!

Sophie Martinez

Sophie is President Martinez's one and only daughter—his princess, you might say. And boy, does she act like it! Sophie expects everyone around her to do whatever she wants, whenever she wants them to do it. Of course, she makes her demands with a sweet smile, and she *can* be reasoned with. Sometimes.

President Martinez

Being the leader of the world's most powerful nation may sound like a stressful job to the average person, but President Martinez is anything but average. He can have fun in any situation. Like when he celebrates by spinning in his desk chair in the Oval Office. You can bet that the White House is not going to be a stodgy, stuffy place during *this* president's term!

Cory's father may be the professional chef in the family, but Cory has picked up a few things from watching his dad in the kitchen. This is one of Cory's favorite recipes to whip up for Newt and Meena. Check it out!

Cory's Chicken Cutlets

INGREDIENTS

- 4 boneless, skinless chicken breasts (about 6 ounces each)
- 2/3 cup fine, dry bread crumbs
- 1/3 cup freshly grated Parmesan cheese
- 2 teaspoons dried basil
- 1 teaspoon dried oregano
- 1/2 teaspoon salt
- 1/8 teaspoon pepper
- 1 egg, beaten
- 2 tablespoons milk
- 1/2 cup flour
- 2 to 4 tablespoons olive oil for frying

DIRECTIONS

1. Rinse the chicken breasts under running water, then place them on a double layer of paper towels and blot dry. (Be sure to wash your hands in soapy water immediately after handling raw chicken; do the same for any cutting boards or utensils that the meat comes in contact with.)

2. Place two of the chicken breasts inside a large, heavy-duty plastic freezer bag. Partially seal the bag, leaving a slight gap so air can escape. Using a rolling pin or the smooth head of a tenderizing mallet, ask a parent to help you pound the meat in even strokes, working from the center out (being careful not to tear the plastic), to a uniform thickness of about 1/2 inch. Repeat this process with the remaining chicken in a new plastic freezer bag.

3. Combine the bread crumbs, Parmesan cheese, basil, oregano, salt, and pepper in a shallow bowl. Stir them to mix. In a separate shallow bowl or pie plate, beat together the egg and milk. Set both of the bowls aside.

4. Spread the flour on a plate. Arrange the breading ingredients in assembly-line fashion in this order: cutlets, flour, egg mixture, crumb mixture, empty plate. Working one piece at a time, cover both sides of the cutlet in the flour, gently shaking off any extra. Next, dip both sides of the floured cutlet in the egg mixture. Finally, coat both sides of the cutlet with the crumb mixture. Repeat the process with the remaining pieces of chicken.

5. Ask a parent for help with the stove. Set a large skillet over medium-high heat and pour in enough olive oil to coat the bottom of the pan. Heat the oil for 2 to 3 minutes, then add the cutlets. (If your pan isn't large enough to cook 4 chicken breasts at once, cook them in batches rather than overcrowd the pan.) Fry each side for 2 ½ to 3 minutes, turning once, until the chicken is browned and cooked through. Remove the cutlets from the heat and serve.

Makes 4 servings.

CHEF CORY'S TIP
Serve these cutlets with a side salad and you've got a delicious and well-balanced meal!

Cory in the House TRIVIA!

A lot of stuff in the White House is top secret. People only find things out on a need-to-know basis—which drives Cory crazy! He always wants to know exactly what's going on. Do you feel you need to know even more about *Cory in the House?* Check out the fun facts below!

Cory in the House is a spin-off of the hit Disney Channel show *That's So Raven*! Kyle Massey landed the role of Cory Baxter on *That's So Raven* back in 2002, when he was only ten years old.

Dwayne "The Rock" Johnson guest-starred as himself on an episode of *Cory in the House*, while Madison Pettis, who plays Sophie Martinez, starred with The Rock in the feature film *The Game Plan*.

Rondell Sheridan, who plays Cory's dad, Victor Baxter, started his career as a stand-up comedian.

Kyle Massey recorded the song "Underdog Raps" for the 2007 feature film *Underdog*.

Jason Dolley, who plays Newt Livingston, starred in the Disney Channel Original Movie *Minutemen* in 2008.

Kyle Massey and Maiara Walsh, who plays Meena Parook, sing the *Cory in the House* theme song.

Jake Thomas, who plays Jason Stickler, starred on another Disney Channel favorite, *Lizzie McGuire*, as Lizzie's little brother, Matt.

Both Madison Pettis and John D'Aquino, who plays President Martinez, took their *Cory in the House* roles on the road and reprised them in a special episode of *Hannah Montana*.

7.6 million viewers tuned in to the first episode of *Cory in the House*!

Ever dreamed of living the glamorous life in an elegant hotel, with twenty-four-hour room service, a pool at your disposal, and fab parties being held every other day? Twins Zack and Cody Martin are living that dream! Ever since their mom, Carey, landed a job as a lounge singer at the fabulous Tipton Hotel in Boston, Massachusetts, the twins have been living like celebs in their very own hotel suite. While the hotel manager, Mr. Moseby, likes to constantly remind them that the hotel does not belong to them, the twins pretty much do whatever they want, wherever they want—until they get snagged, of course. But Zack and Cody don't mind being punished once in a while. After all, what's the point of living in a hotel if you're not going to live it up?

Zack Martin

Zack is all about having fun. He can find it anywhere, anytime—especially living in a place as cool as the Tipton Hotel. He may need to dodge someone to make good on his schemes and plans, whether it's his mom, Carey, the hotel manager, Mr. Moseby, or the crush of his life, candy-counter clerk Maddie Fitzpatrick, but he usually manages to do just what he wants. But more often than not, he ends up getting caught and being grounded, right back on the twenty-third floor.

Luckily, Zack has a partner in crime. His twin brother, Cody, can almost always be talked into helping Zack out with his crazy plans to make some extra cash, throw a secret party, or goof off when he's supposed to be working. Sometimes it takes some convincing, but Zack's a smooth talker and can usually get his brother to see his side of things. Everything's more fun when Cody's in on it with him. After all, two Martins are always better than one! Even when they're grounded.

Cody Martin

Cody's the slightly more responsible one of the Martin twins. He's got a mind for business and loves the satisfaction he gets from a good grade or finishing a hard day's work. Like his brother, Cody likes to have fun. He just puts more thought into the consequences than Zack does. That's not to say he doesn't get sucked into his brother's plans every once in a while, but he's simply less surprised when he and Zack end up grounded.

Cody loves his brother—he just wishes that Zack would listen to reason every once in a while. He also knows that if his brother were less adventurous, they probably wouldn't have as much fun as they do! So he'll keep on listening when Zack comes up with plans to open a teen club or crash exclusive parties at the Tipton. Even the responsible twin has to let loose every once in a while!

London Tipton

London is the superrich and superspoiled daughter of the owner of the Tipton Hotel. She owns several of her own companies, wears all the latest fashions, and regularly appears in magazines and tabloids. She lives for the attention, and she's used to getting her way. London can always be counted on to order the employees of the Tipton around as if they were her own personal assistants. Still, she can be a good friend, too, and will help Zack, Cody, and Maddie out of the occasional jam—*especially* if it also helps her get something she wants.

Maddie Fitzpatrick

Maddie works at the candy counter in the lobby of the Tipton Hotel. She's also been known to pick up extra jobs here or there to make some extra cash, whether it's babysitting Zack and Cody or working as a camp counselor. Unlike London, Maddie wasn't born with millions, so she's always there to point out London's more shallow moments and help her friend treat people with a bit more respect. She also helps Zack and Cody when they get themselves into trouble. She's not only a perfect employee but a loyal friend, too. (Little does she know that Zack has a huge crush on her!)

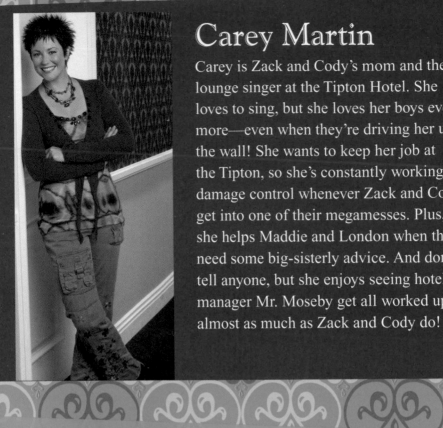

Carey Martin

Carey is Zack and Cody's mom and the lounge singer at the Tipton Hotel. She loves to sing, but she loves her boys even more—even when they're driving her up the wall! She wants to keep her job at the Tipton, so she's constantly working damage control whenever Zack and Cody get into one of their megamesses. Plus, she helps Maddie and London when they need some big-sisterly advice. And don't tell anyone, but she enjoys seeing hotel manager Mr. Moseby get all worked up almost as much as Zack and Cody do!

Mr. Moseby

Mr. Moseby is the manager of the Tipton Hotel. Uptight and snooty, he runs a tight ship—which basically means he has to keep a close watch on Zack and Cody at all times. They've been known to mess up an event or two . . . or ten! But as angry as Mr. Moseby gets with the Martin twins, he always manages to forgive them in the end, usually because they come up with some creative way to make it up to him. Even Mr. Moseby knows that all's well that ends well. As long as it ends with him keeping his job!

Double Trouble

So, you've seen every last episode of *The Suite Life of Zack & Cody* and you think you know all there is to know about the twins and the Tipton Hotel, right? Check out our *Suite Life* quiz and see if you have the key to the penthouse!

1. Zack once bet Cody that he wouldn't be able to spend an entire night in room 613. Why did he think Cody couldn't make it?
   - A. The room is rumored to be haunted.
   - B. The room is home to a rat.
   - C. The room is right next to the noisy elevator.

2. Zack once invited a cat convention to the Tipton on the same day that London was hosting what type of event?
   - A. A sweet-16 birthday bash
   - B. A dog party
   - C. A wedding

3. When London thinks that Carey and Mr. Moseby are too stressed, what activity does she convince them to participate in?
   - A. Swimming
   - B. Race-car driving
   - C. Yoga

4. Why does Zack decide to run against Cody in the eighth-grade student election?
   - A. He thinks he'll make a better president than Cody.
   - B. He wants to impress Maddie.
   - C. He wants to win a trip to Hawaii.

5. What fabulous entrée can Cody cook just as well as Chef Paolo?
   - A. Beef Paolo
   - B. Chicken Paolo
   - C. Veal Parmigiana

6. When Zack and Cody's school holds auditions for *High School Musical*, which part does Cody audition for?
   - A. Chad
   - B. Troy
   - C. Ryan

ANSWERS:

1.A **2.B** **3.C**

4.C **5.B**

6.B

SCORING

Give yourself two points for each correct answer.

0–4 ## Basement Dweller!
You have to do better than that! Until you learn some more Zack and Cody trivia, you'll be living in the icky basement of the Tipton Hotel!

5–9 ## Suite-Sitting!
Nice work! You've earned yourself a cushy suite at the Tipton. Order up some room service and invite all your friends. Just don't let Mr. Moseby find out about it!

10–12 ## Welcome to the Penthouse!
With a score this good, you'll be hanging out in some deluxe digs with London Tipton herself!

The Suite Life of Zack and Cody Trivia

Curious to learn more about Zack and Cody and the rest of the gang from the Tipton Hotel? Check out these fun facts all about the cast and the show!

Dylan and Cole Sprouse, who play Zack and Cody, were born in Italy.

In 2007, *The Suite Life of Zack and Cody* was nominated for Favorite TV Show at the Kids' Choice Awards.

Ashley Tisdale, who plays Maddie Fitzpatrick, also stars as Sharpay Evans in the hit movies *High School Musical* and *High School Musical 2*!

Phil Lewis, who plays Mr. Moseby, also played Principal Tweedy on another Disney Channel favorite, *Lizzie McGuire*.

The twins have their own series of graphic novels titled *47 R.O.N.I.N.*

In 2000, Dylan and Cole were nominated for an MTV Movie Award for Best On-Screen Duo with Adam Sandler, for the movie *Big Daddy*.

Ashley Tisdale once reprised her role of Maddie Fitzpatrick on an episode of *Hannah Montana*.

Running around and having fun at the Tipton Hotel can really work up your appetite. That's why Zack and Cody have come up with four different ways to use the turkey that's always stocked in the Tipton Hotel fridge. Which delicious sandwich will become your new favorite?

Cody and Zack's Top Turkey Sandwiches

THE CAESAR WRAP

Can't decide between a salad and a sandwich? Have both! Line a large flour tortilla with sliced turkey, shredded romaine lettuce, diced tomatoes, shredded Parmesan cheese, and creamy Caesar dressing.

CHEF ZACK'S TIP

Don't try to stuff TOO much into your tortilla, or it'll end up all over your *Suite Life of Zack & Cody* T-shirt!

TURKEY HI-RISE

Build a sandwich the size of the Tipton Hotel! Toast two pieces of your favorite bread, then pile sliced turkey, cooked bacon, lettuce, tomato slices, and mayonnaise between them.

CHEF CODY'S TIP

You can add a third piece of toast in the center to make this sandwich truly tower, but you need a big mouth like Zack's to eat it!

TURKEY REUBEN

Want something that will really fill you up?
Pile turkey, sauerkraut, and Swiss cheese on
rye bread and ask a parent to help you place it
under the broiler or in the toaster oven.
Wait until the cheese melts and then remove it,
letting it cool before eating. Serve with Thousand Island
dressing on the side.

CHEF CODY'S TIP

Between the sauerkraut, the Swiss cheese,
and the dressing, this sandwich can get
kind of smelly. Don't forget to brush
your teeth afterward!

THE CALIFORNIA ROLL-UP

Want to eat like a California
surfer? No problem! Just line
a large flour tortilla with
turkey, lettuce, diced
tomato, avocado, alfalfa
sprouts, and shredded
cheese. Roll it up and enjoy!

CHEF ZACK'S TIP

This is a good sandwich to bring on
an outdoor picnic. It's harder to feel
like a surfer when you're looking out
the window at the latest blizzard to
hit Boston!

When it comes to *Hannah Montana*, you get two times the fun! Not only do you get to know all about Miley Stewart and her regular teen life, but you get to follow pop star Hannah Montana, too! Miley's everyday life is just like yours, with classes, clubs, and cliques. She may not be the most popular girl in school, but what the kids in class don't know is that Miley has a huge secret: regular-girl Miley Stewart is also the superfamous singer Hannah Montana, the star they all worship!

But all the secret-keeping is worth it to Miley. She knows what life would be like if the world found out that she was Hannah Montana: no more hanging at the beach, shopping at the mall, or grabbing pizza with her friends. It would be screaming fans and autograph demands all the time. A girl needs to be able to chill every once in a while—even if it means having to lead a double life.

Want to know even more about Miley and her secret life as Hannah? We've got you covered. On the following pages, you'll find a quiz to test your *Hannah Montana* knowledge, plus trivia on your favorite characters and stars.

Miley Stewart

Miley just might be the luckiest girl in the world. Sometimes she's a regular teenager—hanging out with her friends, Lilly Truscott and Oliver Oken, on the beach, joking around in the halls at school, and going to dances and parties. But when she throws on a blond wig and some blinged-out clothes—*bam!*—she's Hannah Montana! As Hannah, Miley gets to ride in limos, walk the red carpet, and perform for thousands of adoring fans! Sounds perfect, right? Well, it is! Sometimes.

When it comes to keeping her big secret, things gets a bit tricky. Luckily, Miley has her father/manager, Robby Ray Stewart, and her goofy older brother, Jackson, along with Lilly and Oliver, to help maintain her cover. Without their help, it would be a lot harder leading that double life of hers. But as it is, thanks to her friends and family, this girl really *does* have the best of both worlds!

Hannah Montana

Hannah Montana is one of the most famous female pop stars in the world. She has everything a girl could want—a huge closet full of couture fashions, invites to dozens of exclusive parties, plus tons of awards. She's been asked to sing on talk shows, at professional sporting events, and has even headlined a concert tour in Europe. It's a dream life!

Well, sort of. Sometimes, all Hannah wants to do is get away from the spotlight and kick back in her flannel pj's with a scary movie and a big bucket of popcorn. And she'd like to do it *without* the paparazzi snapping her picture through the window. So what's an international superstar to do? Well, live a double life, of course! Hannah has a secret that not even the nosiest reporter has been able to dig up—she's really Miley Stewart, a regular girl who goes to school every day and enjoys all kinds of normal-girl things like hitting the beach with her best friends, Lilly and Oliver, and going to the movies. But not to worry, Hannah's never out of the spotlight for long. She knows her fans need her!

Lilly Truscott

Lilly is Miley's best friend, and the first friend to be let in on Miley's secret. Lilly took the news really well—after a big, huge freak-out! (Lilly can be kind of a drama queen—but always in a fun way.) Never seen without her skateboard or boogie board, Lilly is athletic, funny, and always up for an adventure. She even took on her own secret identity once she found out her best friend was an international pop star! Whenever Lilly goes to concerts or events with Miley, she dresses up as Lola Luftnagle, the pink-haired BFF of Hannah Montana. It's good to be the best friend of a secret star!

Whether Lilly is being Lilly or Lola, she's always there to keep Miley laughing, even when situations get a little bit out of control. She helped Miley handle a poison oak itching fit in the middle of a live TV interview, creatively dodged a sneak attack on Hannah Montana by Oliver Oken, and helped from the audience when Hannah spaced on the words to her own song. Whether they're battling their archenemies at school, Amber Addison and Ashley Dewitt, or fighting off fans on the way to Hannah's limo, Miley and Lilly are there for each other. These best friends are true blue!

Oliver Oken

Oliver is a good friend of Miley's and Lilly's, and he has absolutely no problem making a fool of himself. He had a huge crush on Hannah Montana— *before* he knew that Hannah was really just Miley in disguise, that is! Once Miley revealed her true identity to Oliver, he promptly got over his crush. Thank goodness! Miley would never want to lose a loyal friend like Oliver. Plus, Hannah Montana got to keep him as a fan!

Oliver has proven again and again that he's up for anything. He helped Miley's brother, Jackson, start up his own business at the beach, handcuffed Miley and Lilly together in an effort to help them make up when they were fighting, and even pretended to be Jackson so that he and Miley could sneak out of the house one night. (Not that it was such a good idea!) No friend is more loyal than Oliver Oken. Just don't try chewing gum in front of him. That *really* annoys him!

Jackson Stewart

Jackson is Miley's goofy, scheming, practical-joke-loving older brother. He would do basically anything for a buck, because money means gas in his car, and gas in his car means he can go out on dates. Jackson works a regular job at Rico's Surf Shack on the beach, but he's always looking out for more money-making opportunities. He's tried out everything from opening his own food stand to working as Hannah Montana's assistant—neither of which worked out exactly as he planned. Still, you can bet he's going to keep working at it until he hits the big time!

Jackson loves his little sister, Miley, and would do pretty much anything for her—within reason. Sometimes it annoys him that he has to drive her everywhere and that she seems to get everything she wants. But Jackson will always be there to support both Miley *and* Hannah. He knows what it means to be a good big brother. And if he hides a whoopee cushion under Miley's chair every once in a while, it's all in good fun. Life is quite simple for Jackson, really—until he gets caught scheming, and Mr. Stewart grounds him once again!

Mr. Stewart

Robby Ray Stewart is Miley and Jackson's dad. He not only works as Hannah Montana's manager, but he also writes her songs. Mr. Stewart gave up his glory days as superstar singer Robby Ray in order to hang out with his kids, which is what he loves to do more than anything. Robby likes to think of himself not just as Jackson and Miley's father, but as their friend, too. They can talk to him about anything. And although he does need to ground them every once in a while when they sneak out of the house or run up their "only-for-emergencies" credit cards, he knows how lucky he is to have such a close relationship with his kids.

Of course, being the father of an international pop sensation can be tough. Robby has to decide not just what's best for Miley, but what's best for her career as Hannah Montana. Sometimes he and Miley don't agree on that subject, but they always work it out in the end. Miley knows that her dad has tons of experience in the music business, and Robby knows that Miley is a hard worker who just wants to do the right thing. Plus, at the end of the day, he can always retreat to life's simple pleasures. As long as he's got a guitar to strum, the love of his family, and a piece of chocolate cake waiting for him at the end of the day, Robby's good to go.

Hannah 101

Life can get pretty complicated when you're just a regular girl trying to handle school, friends, and family. So imagine how crazy it is when you're leading a *double* life. Twice the friends, twice the rivals, twice the responsibilities . . . it can be pretty confusing. What's a superfamous pop star to do? Well, don't worry. We won't make your life as complex as Miley's. Instead, we're going to start you out with the basics. Get ready for *Hannah Montana* 101!

1. **When Lilly and Oliver sneak into Hannah's dressing room after a concert, Hannah gives Lilly what as a souvenir?**
   A. A jacket
   B. A towel
   C. A scarf

2. **Lilly has a lucky piece of jewelry, which she lends to Miley. What is it?**
   A. A necklace
   B. A ring
   C. A bracelet

3. **What is Lilly's secret name when she goes undercover as Hannah Montana's best friend?**
   A. Lola
   B. Lara
   C. Orchid

4. **What's the name of the surf shack where Jackson works?**
   A. Ronnie's
   B. Chico's
   C. Rico's

5. **Hannah's strict bodyguard is named:**
   A. Renee
   B. Roxy
   C. Reggie

6. **In the first episode of *Hannah Montana*, what does Miley show Lilly that she's never shown any friend before?**
   A. Her Hannah Montana closet
   B. Her Hannah Montana wig collection
   C. Her belly button

ANSWERS:

1. C **2. C** **3. A** **4. C**

5. B **6. A**

SCORING

Give yourself two points for each correct answer.

0–4
Double-Oh-Nothing!
You are *so* not ready to lead a double life! If you can't even get this basic stuff straight, you'd better just stick with one personality. You'd never be able to keep up with two!

6–8
Double Your Pleasure!
Not bad! You are well on your way to dual-personality status. All you need now is a good wig, a cool stage name, and a very understanding parent to help you keep it all together.

10–12
Undercover Diva!
You've really got your Miley/Hannah info down! You could totally be a cool kid by day/pop star by night. As a matter-of-fact . . . wait . . . Miley, is that you?

HANNAH MONTANA TRIVIA PAGE!

Are you clamoring to go behind the scenes of your favorite double-identity show? Listen up to these backstage bonuses on *Hannah Montana* and its stars!

Miley Cyrus was born in Nashville, Tennessee, on November 23, 1992.

Emily Osment, who plays Lilly Truscott, also starred in *Spy Kids 2: The Island of Lost Dreams* and *Spy Kids 3-D: Game Over*, as Gerti Giggles.

Billy Ray Cyrus, who plays Miley's dad, Robby, on the show, is Miley's father in real life!

Miley Cyrus's real name is Destiny Hope Cyrus. Her father nicknamed her Miley because she was such a smiley baby!

Myley Cyrus was voted Favorite TV Actress and Favorite Female Singer at the 2008 Kids' Choice Awards.

In 2007, Miley Cyrus won two Teen Choice Awards: Choice TV Actress: Comedy, and Choice Summer Artist. The show, *Hannah Montana*, also won the award for Choice TV Show: Comedy.

Mitchell Musso, who plays Oliver Oken, is also the voice of Jeremy Johnson in the new Disney Channel series *Phineas and Ferb*.

Miley already had the part of *Hannah Montana* when Emily came in to audition, and the two of them just clicked. It was clear they were meant to play best friends!

Tickets for the Hannah Montana "Best of Both Worlds" concert tour sold out in just minutes!

Down South, everyone loves a good home-cooked meal, especially one with a little kick! Here's an old family recipe that Miley loves to whip up!

MILEY'S HOMESTYLE CHILI

INGREDIENTS

2	15-ounce cans kidney beans
4	tablespoons olive oil
1 ½	pounds ground beef
2	medium onions, diced
1	medium green bell pepper, diced
2 or 3	garlic cloves, minced
1½ to 2	tablespoons mild chili powder
1	tablespoon cumin
1 ½	tablespoons flour
3	cups chicken or beef stock
1	teaspoon salt
1	28-ounce can crushed tomatoes in puree
1	tablespoon Worcestershire sauce
1 to 2	tablespoons steak sauce
½ to 2	cups additional stock, tomato juice, or water, if needed
	Sour cream
	Cheddar cheese
	Jalapeño peppers (optional)

DIRECTIONS

1. Drain the liquid from the canned beans, then rinse them in a colander.
2. Ask a parent to help you with the stove. Heat 1 tablespoon of the olive oil in a large skillet. Add half of the ground beef and brown it. Using a slotted spoon, transfer the meat to a large soup pot or Dutch oven.

Drain off all but 1 tablespoon of the fat in the skillet, then brown the remaining meat and add it to the pot. Discard all of the fat in the skillet.

3. Pour the remaining 3 tablespoons of olive oil into the empty skillet. Add the onions and peppers and sauté them over medium heat for 6 minutes, stirring often. Stir in the garlic and cook 2 minutes more.

4. Sprinkle the chili powder, cumin, and flour over the vegetables in the skillet and sauté for 1 minute more, stirring nonstop. Stir in 1 cup of the stock and cook for 1 minute. Transfer the contents of the skillet to the pot, along with the salt, crushed tomatoes, Worcestershire sauce, and steak sauce. Stir in the remaining 2 cups of stock and the beans.

5. Bring the chili to a low boil, stirring occasionally. Reduce the heat, cover, and simmer for 1 to 1 ½ hours, stirring occasionally. When done, the chili should be thick, but still somewhat soupy. If it starts to get too thick, add extra stock, tomato juice, or water. Serve with a dollop of sour cream, a sprinkle of cheddar cheese, and, if desired, jalapeño peppers.

Makes 8 or more servings.

CHEF MILEY'S TIP:
Serve the chili up with cornbread to complete this yummy down-home meal! (You can make the cornbread from a simple, store-bought mix or buy it pre-made.)

Wizards
OF WAVERLY PLACE

Ever wish you could snap your fingers to magically finish your homework? Or snap them again and find your bedroom suddenly clean? Alex Russo and her brothers, Justin and Max, can—or they could, if their parents would let them use their magic for daily dilemmas! The only place they *are* allowed to use their powers is in the lair, where their dad, Jerry, teaches them all about magic wands, crystal balls, and magic spells. Each of the Russo kids wants to learn as much magic as they can, because one day they will have to take a test to see which one of them gets to keep their powers! Only one child in each wizard family gets to keep their magic skills into adulthood, so the Russo kids are always competing—except when they're helping each other out.

Alex Russo

Alex is the middle child of the Russo family and daddy's little girl. All she wants is to be allowed to use her magic to make her life a bit easier, but her parents have strict rules about spells and charms. They don't want her to rely too much on magic, because they want her to learn how to live in the world without it. Sometimes it's just too tempting, though, and she finds herself casting a spell to magically change her outfit or help one of her brothers out of a jam. After all, what's the point of being a wizard if you can't put your powers to good use?

Justin Russo

Justin is the oldest child in the family and his nickname could be Mr. Responsible. He's a good student both in his regular classes and in the lair, where he and his siblings learn all about their powers. He also runs a tutoring business and is the least likely of the Russo kids to break the no-magic rule. But he does enjoy standing by and watching everything unravel whenever Alex or Max try out a spell. He is only human, after all. Well, human *and* wizard.

Max Russo

Max is the youngest of the Russo kids, and the most eager to try anything and everything—at *least* once. Whether it's inventing wild-and-crazy sandwich recipes, testing out spells with his new magic wand, or trying to get the info for his Mars project *directly* from Mars, Max is always ready for adventure!

Harper Evans

Harper is Alex's BFF. She has a quirky sense of style, loves to make her own clothes, and doesn't care much about what other people think of her. She doesn't know that her best friend has magical powers, but she *does* know pretty much everything else about Alex, and is always there for her—especially when Alex's archenemy, Gigi, starts causing trouble!

Jerry Russo

Jerry has a lot of responsibilities. Not only is he the father to three budding wizards, but he also teaches their wizard class and helps run the family business, The Waverly Sub Station. He used to have magical powers when he was a kid, but lost them when he married a mortal, Theresa Russo. Now Jerry is determined that all his kids will learn as much magic as possible, so that each of them will have a fair shot at keeping their powers. Normally he freaks out when one of his kids breaks his no-magic-outside-the-lair rule, but he's always there to help them clean up their magical messes. After all, he does remember what it was like to be a kid with powers: lots of fun!

Theresa Russo

Theresa is mother to the Russo kids and helps her husband, Jerry, run The Waverly Sub Station. She never had magical powers herself, but she *was* young once, so she's always there to help her kids out with their nonmagical issues. Whether it's helping Justin with girl troubles, shopping with Alex, or coaching Max through his homework, Theresa loves to help out her kids. She allows them to practice magic but tries to keep it to a minimum so they can have a normal life, too.

WIZARDS OF WAVERLY PLACE 101

Think you've got every magical moment of *Wizards of Waverly Place* memorized? Well, let's find out! Take our whiz quiz and see just how magical your mental powers are!

1. Which of these names does Justin choose to be his new nickname?

A. J-Dog
B. The J-Man
C. The Jayster

2. What sports team wants to use Max's sandwich at their games?

A. The New York Mets
B. The New York Yankees
C. The New York Giants

3. What is the name of Justin's "Goth" girlfriend?

A. Miranda
B. Matilda
C. Maureen

4. What is the one thing you cannot give to Pocket Elves?

A. Sodas
B. Sandwiches
C. Chocolate

5. Which spell does Alex cast on Harper to help her become a better waitress?
   A. The Duplication Spell
   B. The Serving-Wench Spell
   C. The Time-Rewinding Spell

7. What does Alex find in the basement that her parents didn't want her to know about?
   A. A magic rug/carpet
   B. Her dad's baseball-glove chair
   C. Her mom's guitar

6. Alex and Gigi have been fighting since which grade?
   A. Fourth
   B. Seventh
   C. Kindergarten

8. What is the name of the new restaurant Riley invites Alex to for dinner?
   A. Medium Rare
   B. Surburban Outfitters
   C. The Shake Shack

ANSWERS:

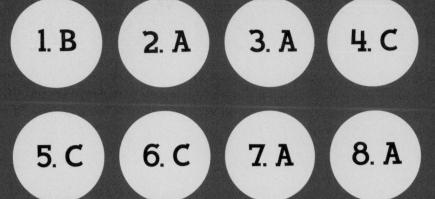

1. B 2. A 3. A 4. C

5. C 6. C 7. A 8. A

SCORING:

Give yourself two points for each correct answer.

0-4 Novice Wizard

You really haven't been doing your studying outside the lair. Better buckle down or you'll never get to use that new wand you ordered!

5-9 Average Wizard

You've got most of your wizard knowledge down, but the trickier stuff is still stumping you. Don't worry. All it will take is a few extra wizard classes to get you up to speed!

10-16 Expert Wizard

You are a true expert on all things *Wizards of Waverly Place*! We're so impressed we might even let you use magic outside the lair! Just kidding!

Wizards of Waverly Place Trivia!

Want to know even more about *Wizards of Waverly Place*? All you've got to do is snap your fingers! Oh, and read our trivia tidbits below.

Selena Gomez, who plays Alex Russo, played Hannah Montana's pop-star rival Mikayla on two episodes of *Hannah Montana*!

In-between scenes of the show, the Russo siblings are seen jumping up and down on the screen.

David Henrie, who plays Justin Russo, and Jennifer Stone, who plays Harper Evans, starred in the Disney Channel Original Movie *Dadnapped*.

Selena says the spell she would most like to be able to use in real life is the Time Rewinding spell, which allows wizards' to rewind time and get a second chance.

The theme song for the show, "Everything is Not What it Seems" is performed by Selena Gomez.

BEWITCHING BLUEBERRY PANCAKES

Everyone knows it's important to eat a good breakfast, especially when you're a wizard-in-training! Those spells take lots of energy to cast—especially the "Conjure Pancakes" spell that Alex uses when she gets to school and realizes that she's skipped breakfast! These are her favorite pancakes.

INGREDIENTS

1 3/4 cups flour
  2 tablespoons sugar
  1 teaspoon baking powder
1/2 teaspoon baking soda
1/2 teaspoon salt
1/4 teaspoon nutmeg
  2 eggs
  1 cup milk
  1 cup sour cream
1/4 cup melted butter or vegetable oil, plus extra for the pan
1/2 teaspoon vanilla extract
1/2 teaspoon finely grated lemon zest
1 1/2 cups fresh blueberries

DIRECTIONS

1. Sift the flour, sugar, baking powder, baking soda, salt, and nutmeg into a large mixing bowl.
2. In a separate large bowl, lightly whisk the eggs. Add the milk, sour cream, melted butter (or oil), and vanilla extract and whisk to blend.
3. Make a well in the dry ingredients and pour the liquid mixture into it. Vigorously whisk the ingredients until just blended (about 10 seconds).

4. Add the lemon zest and blueberries and gently fold them into the batter with a rubber spatula.

5. Ask a parent to help you heat a large frying pan or skillet over medium heat for 3 to 4 minutes. Then pour in enough butter to coat the surface. Using a pot holder to grasp the pan handle with both hands, gently swirl the skillet around to evenly distribute the butter.

6. For each pancake, ladle about $\frac{1}{4}$ cup of batter onto the hot skillet.

7. Cook the pancakes on one side until the bubbles that form on the top burst. Then flip and cook until the bottoms are golden brown.

8. Serve the pancakes at once, preferably on warm plates. Top with butter and maple syrup.

Makes about 15 pancakes.

CHEF ALEX'S TIP:
Never let your little brother flip the pancakes. They may end up stuck to the ceiling!

CAMP ROCK

The Ultimate Music Experience

The woods are filling up with the sounds of music. When Mitchie Torres gets the chance to attend Camp Rock, *the* place for aspiring musicians, she is in for the best summer of her life! Join her, Shane Gray, and the rest of the campers as they rock out in the sure-to-be hit movie coming to Disney Channel this summer!

Classes May Include:

★ Rock 'n' Roll Roots

★ Hip-Hop Nation

★ A Little Bit Country

★ R&B Rhythms

★ Pop-Star Power

Plus many, many more! And at this rockin' camp, you never know who your instructor might be!

SIGN UP TODAY! Space is limited and filling up fast!

CAMP IT UP

We'll pack your summer with fun, friends, and music!
Enjoy:
Jam Sessions!
Concerts!
Campfires!
Boat Rides!
Swimming!

"STUFF LIKE FIGHTING A MUMMY...

"...OR CLIMBING UP THE *EIFFEL TOWER*...

"...OR SURFING TIDAL WAVES, OR--"

HEY, WHERE'S PERRY?

REMEMBER, THE *FAMILY* YOU LIVE WITH MUST *NEVER* SUSPECT THAT YOU ARE WORKING FOR THE GOVERNMENT!

WELL, FERB-- WHAT ARE WE GOING TO DO *TOMORROW?*

THE BEGINNING!

learned how to make Miley's Homestyle Chili, caught the latest buzz about new shows like *Phineas and Ferb*, rocked out with *Hannah Montana*, and answered all of the trivia about *Wizards of Waverly Place* correctly, you've proven yourself to be the ultimate fan! Tune into the Disney Channel to catch all of your favorite shows, and remember, Disney Channel rocks!